MW01520644

TRICKSTER TALES *for* TELLING

A Collection of West African Tales for Call-and-Response Storytelling

Abimbola Gbemi Alao

Lampo Educational Services

To choë & Alice
Best Wishes

3/3/16

First published in 2016 by Lampo Educational Services

Copyright © 2016 Abimbola Gbemi Alao.

The right of Abimbola Gbemi Alao to be identified as the author of this work has been asserted in accordance with the Copyright, Designs and Patents Act of 1988.

All rights reserved. No part of this publication may be reproduced, stored in a retrieval system, or transmitted, in any form or by any means, electronic, mechanical, photocopying or otherwise, without the prior permission of the publisher, nor be otherwise circulated in any form of binding or cover other than that in which it is published.

This is a work of fiction, and any resemblance to persons, living or dead, is purely coincidental.

ISBN: 978-0-9546255-4-2

www.lampoeducation.org

"Each of us has been designed for one of two immortal functions, as either a storyteller or as a cross-legged listener to tales of wonder, love and daring. When we cease to tell or listen, then we no longer exist as a people. Dead men tell no tales."

Bryce Courtenay 'A Recipe for dreaming'

"Abimbola is a storyteller through and through. She has a magical touch with words and tells stories that people want to listen to, and which have them hooked from beginning to end. In this book she shares some of her lively tales of sneaky tricksters, which will keep audiences hanging on to find out if they get their comeuppance. It is an excellent resource for professional and amateur storytellers."

Alison Gagg (Education Manager, Buckfast Abbey)

"Abimbola guides us skillfully into West African culture with her lively retelling of trickster tales. The stories are filled with captivating dilemmas, layered meanings and plenty of opportunity for audience participation! These fables are a wonderful way to engage children during assemblies. They also work well incorporated into literacy lessons and they offer easy cross-curricula links, along with rich opportunities for 'Talk for Writing'. I'm already looking forward to what I'm sure will be a memorable storytelling experience with my class."

Anna Payne (Year 1 Class Teacher, Abbey School)

"Abimbola has combined these traditional tales with her unique magic and rhythm. Trickster tales are always fun with their mischievous, cunning characters. Storyteller Abi doesn't miss a chance at a thoughtful ending; the stories, like the tunes, stick in the memory. These call-and-answer tales are linked to the chants and songs available online and they will transport a class full of children away on an African adventure."

Amy Robinson (Writer, Storyteller and Ventriloquist)

"Abimbola takes us right into the imaginative landscape of traditional Yoruba culture to meet notorious trickster, Ijapa the Tortoise. These wise and witty call and response stories leap off the page to stimulate our senses, through movement, gesture, percussion, chanting and song."

David Heathfield (Storyteller Writer and Lecturer)

"Alao's collection of tales uses humour to create memorable moral lessons. The ideas in these stories are poignant and sophisticated; however, life issues are presented in an accessible way. I love the use of allegory, particularly in 'The Tortoise, the Elephant and the Hippopotamus'. This is a great resource for storytellers and teachers."

Grace Yesufu (Assistant Head Teacher: English and Literacy, The John Warner School)

"With this set of inspiring tales, Alao has provided storytellers with a valuable, thought-provoking resource that will enable all participants in their sessions to fully engage on a range of levels."

Kitty Heardman (English Language and Music Educator)

"This book reflects Abimbola's unique approach to storytelling. Her techniques are truly inspirational!"

Debbie Burman (English Deputy Manager, Stoke Damerel Community College)

TABLE OF
CONTENTS

INTRODUCTION

I grew up in Nigeria, where the oral tradition thrives. My storytelling journey began around four decades ago, when three noble women laid a firm foundation for my current career. The first woman was my maternal grandmother, who told real life stories, some of which were about her experiences as a woman raising her children in a polygamous home.

The second person was my mother, who told us Bible narratives every night before we went to bed. She built the first bookshelf we had in our living room and filled it with books of all kinds, many of which she got from a charity organisation based at the Cocoa House in Ibadan.

The third woman who was instrumental in stirring my passion for storytelling was a nanny that we had when I was eight years old. Every night, when she came back from her evening classes, she told my siblings and me fictional stories in nearly every genre of the oral tradition, performing them with songs and chants.

These three women introduced me to different forms of

storytelling. My mother and grandmother have since passed away and I haven't heard from the nanny since 1975, but I will forever be grateful to them. I am also indebted to my father, whose decision not to buy a television set for us when we were young was instrumental in helping me develop my skill as a storyteller.

When the nanny left our house, I stepped into her shoes as the family storyteller. Every evening after school and during the holidays, I told stories to my siblings and the children who lived in our neighbourhood. I told ones that I had heard, plus ones I had read in books. I also made up sagas, which I relayed over a long period of time, encouraging my exuberant audience to participate in the songs and movement. We had so much fun.

There were other griots and storytellers whose contagious enthusiasm for the oral tradition helped me to build on the foundation; these people generously shared their repertoire of stories; they were my heroes.

Today, I am privileged to run training sessions and workshops for teachers, outdoor educators and storytellers in various settings. I always ask my audience what they hope to learn from my workshops. All good storytellers want to engage effectively with their audience because that is what creates a memorable experience.

One of the ways in which I engage with my audience and keep them immersed in my stories is by using the call-and-response method. This involves the storyteller starting a song (this is the call) and the audience singing the chorus, thereby 'responding' to the tale they are hearing. In my book entitled 'How to Enhance Your Storytelling with Music', there are a few tips on how to create a memorable and engaging storytelling event using music and rhythm.

In today's 'fast-paced' society, an audience will have been exposed to first-rate entertainment through films, theatre or television; it may take more than straightforward narration to hold their attention. Call-and-response narrative reinforces the absence of the 'fourth wall' in storytelling, and it creates rapport between tellers and listeners. In this collection, the focus is on trickster tales.

I heard these stories when I was growing up in Nigeria and I thoroughly enjoyed them. Unfortunately, many of them are only available as oral narratives; they were not recorded in books, so I had to rely on my imagination each time I tried to retell them. A few years ago, I decided to write and publish some of them, so that the next generation of storytellers could access the tales of Ijapa the tortoise.

The first part of the journey was to translate the original stories from Yoruba to English, in order to share them with a wider, non-Yoruba speaking audience. I have translated several books for major publishers, therefore, I thought this project would be easy but I soon realised that it was no mean feat. Nevertheless, after many months, I finished the first part and moved on to adaptation. This also had its own challenges; one of them was how to write the tales to suit a modern audience. To overcome this challenge, I decided to modify the stories and I also wrote brand new scenes, characters and plots. I enjoyed recreating each of these stories and giving them a contemporary twist; I hope you will also enjoy them.

How to Use This Book

All the stories in this book are mainly for retelling, hence the oral tradition style. They can be used in a variety of ways as shown below:

1. Storytellers, therapists and parents can learn the stories and retell them.

2. Teachers can use the collection as a co-curricular resource to generate discussion for subjects such as: Geography, Science, Religious Studies, Personal, Social and Health Education (PSHE), Literacy and Music. For example, I use 'The Tortoise and the Pig' story to explore the different seasons of the year in various parts of the world, while 'The Tortoise and the Gelada Baboon' is great for generating discussion on rare species and their habitats.

3. The tales of Ijapa the trickster are great around campfires and outdoor trips; therefore, this collection is a useful resource for youth and community workers, and forest school practitioners. The stories can also be used to explore topics such as: bullying, friendship, selfishness, boldness, courage, greed, laziness or disobedience.

4. Writers who wish to create depth in their writing by exploring the hypodiegetic level may also find these stories useful. This level of narration is achieved when characters tell smaller narratives within the main story, thereby creating an embedded or frame narrative. Some

authors who used frame narratives include: F. Scott Fitzgerald in 'The Great Gatsby', Chinua Achebe in 'Things fall Apart' and Wole Soyinka in his play, 'Death and the King's Horseman'. However, this is not only applicable to fiction. Non-fiction writers can also use relevant tales to plant powerful images in the minds of their readers and help them to connect with their ideas.

5. Public or motivational speakers can also use the stories as anecdotes or exemplum.

Why Trickster Tales?

Over the last three decades, I have translated, adapted and retold fairy tales, folk tales, parables and trickster tales. However, I find trickster tales the most intriguing, as they usually feature anthropomorphised animals. In Native American culture, the trickster, Coyote, has magical powers. In parts of Europe and South America, the trickster is often a wolf or fox, while in West Africa, Ijapa the tortoise and Anansi the spider are notable tricksters and they rely on rhetoric and cunningness.

The structure of many of these tales is accessible, although the narratives are complex and versatile. The tales are widespread and found in nearly every culture due to the ancient wisdom that they possess.

I'd like to make a note here that my focus, in this book, is mainly on trickster fables, featuring anthropomorphised West African tricksters, and not on mythological characters that operate in the terrain of polytheism.

I love trickster tales because they give me the opportunity to engage creatively with my audience for the following reasons:

1. Tricksters Are Tenacious

Many of the West African trickster tales start off as a quest and there is usually a problem. For example, there may be famine in the trickster's country and he may face a tough challenge. Nevertheless, he is non-relenting in his quest and will do everything he can to get what he wants. An example of such is the story 'The Tortoise and the Rabbit'.

The tales of Anansi the trickster are popular in the Caribbean, though they originated from Ghana. They were brought to the Caribbean during the Trans-Atlantic Slave Trade, and the slaves on the plantations told these stories as a way to outwit their cruel masters. These storytellers identified with the weak and seemingly helpless tricksters, who used manipulative words to map their way out of adversity. The tenacity of the trickster was a prominent and recurrent theme in 'Plantation Tales'.

2. The Tales Are Complex

Our experiences in life are not linear; they are full of twists and turns. There are times to be brave and times to be cautious and apply wisdom. Trickster tales mirror this complexity and they can be likened to instruction manuals on the essence of life and wisdom. "The many roles of the trickster and his antagonists create a complex suturing of layers of social meanings in the structure of the tales... This is manifested in his Siamese disposition to disrupt and reorganise" (Sekoni 1994: p 10 & 23.)[1]. The ambivalence and complexity of these tales help to captivate an audience and retain their attention.

Trickster tales are not just about morals. In many stories, Ijapa the tortoise is amoral, and he lacks emotional intelligence. He is always at the mercy of his appetite or lust, yet "through his actions, all values come into being". (Reesman 2001, p xii)[2]. Am I encouraging my audiences to be amoral? Absolutely not! Nevertheless, "people recognise the need to devise strategies to cope with the many and sundry obstacles that they encounter as they go through life" (Owomoyela 1997 p xiv)[3].

3. Tricksters Are Great Orators

A major characteristic of West African tricksters is their physical form. Some of them, like the tortoise and spider, seem weak or helpless; however, appearances can be deceptive and the tricksters know their limitations, hence their reliance on rhetoric. Ijapa the tortoise moves at a very slow pace and he carries a huge shell on his back, yet he is able to bring mighty animals like hippopotamuses, elephants and lions to their knees by using persuasive words and actions.

4. Tricksters Are Irrepressible

Tricksters like Ijapa do not fear borders. They know how to fearlessly cross them and are able to challenge the norms and prejudices in their society. The irrepressible nature of the

---

1 Sekoni, R 1994 Folk Poetics: A Socio-semiotic Study of Yoruba Trickster Tales Greenwood Press

2 Reesman J. 2001 Trickster Lives: Culture and Myth in American Fiction. University of Georgia Press

3 Owomoyela, O. 1997 Yoruba Trickster Tales. University of Nebraska Press

7

trickster endears him to his fans. He teaches them how to navigate the treacherous labyrinths of life, or how to function in the midst of chaos rather than give in to despondency. Lovers of these tales learn how to get unstuck from life's muddy traps, even when the situations they face seem hopeless.

When I was in young, I was bullied and I dreaded going to school because the bullies took my lunch money and sometimes beat me up. The other students saw what was happening but did nothing, and I was too frightened to tell my parents. I knew they would come to the school, and I thought that would make matters worse.

I was shy and didn't engage with my classmates, but I noticed that our class teacher loved students who were clever and quiet. The only thing I had going for me at that time was my quietness. Before long, the teacher noticed I was responsible enough to be given the job of writing down the names of 'noise-makers' any time she went out of the class. Well, that was my breakthrough; I had the pen and paper. Suddenly, boys and girls who wouldn't say a word to me in class started coming to my desk to give their advice on whose names should or shouldn't be on my paper. That was the first time a teacher in school gave me the opportunity to do anything, even if it was as insignificant as writing down names.

Bullying is a terrible offence. It can disrupt a child's life, and I'm not in any way trying to make light of it. However, we often focus on bullies and their bad ways, but we also need to empower the victims. In my booklet, 'How To Enhance Your Storytelling With Music', I shared the story of 'Aja the dancing dog'. Aja was a bobtail that voiced his apprehension about going to school, but his mother quickly helped him to refocus on his talents instead of his disability.

People often tell victims of bullying to 'stand up for themselves', but many of them became victims in the first place because they didn't know exactly how to do that; hence such advice falls on deaf ears. In addition to encouraging people to speak up about abuse, it is important to help them focus on what they are good at doing; that may boost their confidence.

As a little girl, I used to imagine the bullies as powerful, and I saw myself as a tiny cockroach that could be snuffed out at any moment; however, the situation changed when I got the teacher's attention and subsequently made more friends. I gradually became bolder and I even raised my hand to answer questions in class.

I love trickster tales because the protagonists are usually small and weak, yet they are able to overcome terrible situations. Also, these anthropomorphised animals don't recoil into their shells and throw pity parties, nor do they succumb to depression. They use their imagination to 'plot' their way out of negative situations.

As I watch the tricksters negotiate the bends and curves of life, I am sometimes amused at their quick wit, but I also see how their actions mirror the natural world. It is rare to find a creature that sits by and allows itself to be destroyed by another, without putting up a fight. Whether we are battling with bullies, harsh weather conditions or any form of danger, we can learn survival skills from the tricksters. They teach us how to challenge the negative mind chatter and mini narratives that occupy our subconscious and render us helpless and immobile. The tricksters are never immobile; they are too busy planning and plotting to give in to despondency.

Many years ago, when I discovered the tales of Ijapa, I couldn't get enough of them. Could it be that I located myself in these stories or sought refuge in them when the fear of bullies was overwhelming?

5. Trickster Tales Have Multi-Layered Messages

The messages in trickster tales are multi-layered. On one level, they are encapsulated in the Yoruba proverb *'Ogbon ju agbara'* – 'Wisdom is greater than physical strength'. On another level, there is the 'closure moral'. How does a storyteller bring closure to a tale in which the selfish or evil deeds of the trickster may have caused emotional trauma to other characters? This is where trickster tales provide the opportunity for creative engagement. There are a few ways by which I end such tales during my performances. I may leave a story in the unsteady hands of a cliffhanger and ask my audience to tell their own version of the end. This encourages children to engage with the open-ended structure of my story and be active participants in the construction of meaning as they become open to new ideas.

The Aim Of This Collection Of Tales

My aim is to share with you some of the tales that I use for my performance storytelling. Many of them are original tales that I learned from griots in Nigeria. I have translated each one and rewritten them to be enjoyed by a modern audience.

I have also included a few songs that I use for call-and-response storytelling. These are Yoruba playground songs and lullabies that have been passed down from generation to generation. You can listen to or download them from this link: www.storytellerabi.bandcamp.com.

I enjoy using the stories in this collection in various creative ways. I hope you will also enjoy telling them and singing with your audience!

THE TORTOISE
AND THE RABBIT

Many years ago, a terrible drought hit an ancient animal kingdom. It had not rained for two years and all the crops were dead. The animals hoped and prayed for an end to the drought, but the sky was no longer able to gather enough clouds and the rains did not come.

The famine was having a devastating effect on all the animals, so much so that Ijapa, the tortoise, who lived on the outskirts of the village with his family, could no longer trick others into parting with the little rations of food they possessed.

One morning, a very tired and hungry Ijapa left his house with the intention of searching the marketplace for scraps of food. When he arrived, he saw that there wasn't any food. Just as he was about to return home he saw Ehoro, the rabbit, hopping towards the market. There was something strange about Ehoro; he looked radiant, well-fed and full of exuberance. Ijapa was curious. *Why is Ehoro looking so well and I am so hungry?* he thought. He decided to approach the rabbit with his head bowed, as if he was very sad. Then he began to cry. When Ehoro saw Ijapa and he rushed towards him.

"What is wrong, my friend?" the rabbit asked kindly.

"My father is ill and my wife is expecting our third child, but she is so hungry that I fear for her and the baby's health," Ijapa answered. "As if that were not enough, last night I heard that my mother-in-law is dying of starvation. I feel terrible because there is nothing I can do!"

Initially, Ehoro was suspicious; it was well known that the tortoise was sly and could not always be trusted. But Ijapa was an excellent performer and soon won the rabbit's sympathy.

"Meet me at Ore Brook after dark," said Ehoro. "I will help you."

Soon it was night and Ijapa set out into the darkness to find Ehoro waiting at the brook. Once they had said their hellos, both animals made their way into the deep forest; the rabbit led the way while the tortoise followed closely behind.

Before long, they came to a narrow path that led to an open clearing among the trees in the middle of the forest. The rabbit stopped, pulled the tortoise to his side and whispered, "what you are about to see must be kept a secret; do you understand?" The tortoise nodded and the rabbit cupped his hands around his mouth and began to sing...

Song

Call:	*Kulumbu yeye oyeye kulumbu*
Response:	*Kulumbu yeye oyeye kulumbu*
Call:	*A o fotun gbomo jo*
Response:	*Kulumbu yeye oyeye kulumbu*

Call:	*A o fosi gbomo pon*
Response:	*Kulumbu yeye oyeye kulumbu*

Translation

Call:	*Bouncy baby, Bouncy baby*
Response:	*Bouncy baby, Bouncy baby*
Call:	*I will place you on my right arm and dance with you*
Response:	*Bouncy baby, Bouncy baby*
Call:	*I will place you on my left arm and dance with you*
Response:	*Bouncy baby, Bouncy baby*

You can listen to or download the song from:
www.storytellerabi.bandcamp.com

Suddenly, a long white rope descended from the sky. Ehoro grabbed the rope and began to climb it. After hesitating for just a moment, Ijapa also took hold of the rope and followed the rabbit up into the night sky.

The rabbit and the tortoise climbed and climbed until they got to the very top of the rope where there was a magnificent fluffy cloud, shaped like a door. The door opened and there stood a friendly old rabbit with a smile upon her face.

"Mother!" exclaimed Ehoro in a joyful voice as he embraced the old rabbit. "This is my friend, Ijapa. He has come for supper." Ehoro's mother held out her hand and gave the tortoise a warm handshake. "Come in and eat with us," she said. "I have just set the table."

The sight that met Ijapa's eyes made him gasp. There was a large table laden with the most sumptuous food he had ever seen. There were exotic fruits and fresh fish of all types. There was also rice, yam and mouth-watering soup. The tortoise whistled quietly.

"Where did you find all this food?" he whispered to Ehoro, but the rabbit ignored him and gave him a stern look. "Ijapa, please join us at the table," he said eventually. The hungry tortoise dug in immediately and ate everything that he could get his hands on.

"Don't eat too much," Ehoro warned, "or you will not be able to go down the rope and walk back to the village." The tortoise continued to eat until eventually he slumped back in his chair and gazed dozily around the room, his belly protruding like a huge balloon. After they had rested for a while, Ehoro decided that it was time to return home. Ijapa rubbed his large belly, got to his feet very slowly, and made his way to the door.

"Aren't you going to take some food back home for your family?" Ehoro's mother asked Ijapa.

"No thank you," replied Ijapa, "my belly is full and I feel so heavy that I cannot carry any food with me."

Ehoro's mother let down the rope and the rabbit and the tortoise descended back into the forest and went their separate ways.

When Ijapa got home, his family was asleep so he tiptoed into his bed, covered himself up with his blanket, and fell into a deep twelve-hour sleep. When he eventually woke up, he was very hungry. *I need food*, he thought to himself. *I need food and I need it now.* It was then that Ijapa had an idea. *I will go*

back to Ehoro's house while he is still at work. I will think of
some lies to tell his mother when she lets down the rope, and I
will fill my belly once again.

When Ijapa arrived at the open space in the forest, he
cleared his throat and began to sing the same song that Ehoro
had sung the previous night...

Song

Call:	*Kulumbu yeye oyeye kulumbu*
Response:	*Kulumbu yeye oyeye kulumbu*
Call:	*A o fotun gbomo jo*
Response:	*Kulumbu yeye oyeye kulumbu*
Call:	*A o fosi gbomo pon*
Response:	*Kulumbu yeye oyeye kulumbu*

The trouble was, Ijapa had a rather husky voice and the song
did not sound as beautiful or as heartfelt as when it was sung
by Ehoro.

That does not sound like my son, thought Ehoro's mother.
The old rabbit hesitated for a moment, but eventually she let
down the rope. *Perhaps he has caught a cold*, she thought as
she lowered the rope into the clearing below.

The mischievous tortoise was delighted to see the rope
fall to the ground; he quickly grabbed it with both hands
and began to climb as fast as he could. Ijapa was half way up
the rope when he heard a voice shouting from the forest
below.

"Hey, where do you think you're going? Come back down
at once!" It was Ehoro, and he sounded very angry. "Mother,

we've been tricked!" he shouted. Still Ijapa climbed, his mind full of thoughts of the feast awaiting him above. Ehoro called out to his mother again, but nothing happened. Undeterred, the tortoise continued to climb up the rope into the clouds. Ehoro cleared his throat, took a very deep breath, and sang to his mother up in the clouds...

Song

Call:	*Kulumbu yeye oyeye kulumbu*
Response:	*Kulumbu yeye oyeye kulumbu*
Call:	*A o fotun gbomo jo*
Response:	*Kulumbu yeye oyeye kulumbu*
Call:	*A o fosi gbomo pon*
Response:	*Kulumbu yeye oyeye kulumbu*

When Ehoro's mother heard her son's voice she exclaimed, "Now that is my son! But who was the first caller?" The old rabbit peered through the clouds to see what was happening below and she saw the tortoise climbing towards her.

"Mother!" shouted Ehoro from down below, "cut the rope!" He feared that Ijapa might harm his mother.

The old rabbit fetched a large carving knife and cut at the rope. At first it seemed as if it was made of iron and that the knife would have no effect at all, but Ehoro's mother continued to hack at the rope with all her might and soon there was only a very thin strand left for the tortoise to hang onto. The old rabbit gave the rope one final hack with the knife and *whooooaaaahhhh*! Ijapa went tumbling down towards the forest below.

The winds carried Ijapa back and forth, tossing him around in the sky until he landed heavily on his back. Unfortunately for him, the only thing to cushion his fall was a big rock on the forest floor. As he landed on the rock, Ijapa's shell cracked in so many places that it ended up looking like a jigsaw puzzle. He was in so much agony that he passed out.

The tortoise woke up many hours later, still very dazed. He was able to move, though, and found that he was not in very much pain after all. His shell, however, remained like a jigsaw puzzle and would never again return to the lovely smooth and round shape that it was before the fall.

THE TORTOISE
AND THE
ONE-EYED LION

Once upon a time, there was a village called Adawa, where all the animals lived together peacefully. The village was situated at the foot of Mount Adawa; a spring flowed through it that gave the inhabitants water throughout the year, even during the dry season.

One day, on a dark moonless night, the animals heard a strange, loud roar, like the rumbling of thunder. It was a piercing sound with an icy shrill.

"It's the one-eyed lion that lives on Mount Adawa!" said the owl.

"Is he still alive?" the bush rat asked. "We heard that he died many years ago."

Again, the booming noise echoed through the village. "I am the king of the mountains," the lion roared. That sent the animals sprawling in various directions.

"I'm right; it's coming from the mountains; the one-eyed lion is awake," said the owl. Before he finished speaking, the earth beneath them began to shake and all the animals made a dash for their homes. Soon, the rumbling stopped and everything went back to normal, but the village remained quiet.

The following day, the owl called the animals to a meeting at the village centre. When everyone had gathered, he said, "My friends, strange things are happening in our village and we really need to do something about it. Yesterday, we all heard the rumbling and the roar of the one-eyed lion. That can only mean one thing."

"What?" asked the monkey.

"Evil," the owl replied.

"What shall we do?" asked the bush rat almost in a whisper. "The one-eyed lion is evil, oh he's so evil…"

"Since the owl knows so much about the one-eyed lion who lives on the mountain, why doesn't he go and ask him what he wants?" the monkey interrupted. All the animals nodded in agreement and the owl reluctantly agreed to fly out to the mountain. The animals waited patiently for him and later that evening he came back with a message from the lion.

"It's bad news," the owl announced. "The one-eyed lion wants us to draw up a food rota. He said we must come to him one by one so he can eat us for dinner."

"What a terrible idea," said the monkey. "Why should…"

"Please be quiet for a minute and let me finish my message!" the owl scolded, before continuing with his story. "According to the lion, if we come to him on a regular basis, he won't need to roar loudly and send us all into a panic, and he won't hunt us down fiercely. He will stay on the mountain and wait patiently for his dinner. So all we need to do is go to him one by one."

"Ha! He must be out of his miserable mind. He is not eating me for dinner and that's that!" yelled the monkey, and he climbed a tree and left the other animals dumbfounded at the news that the owl had brought to them. They were paralysed with fear because they knew that they wouldn't be able to escape the fierce lion. If they didn't go to him, he would eventually hunt them down one by one. The question on everyone's mind was, who will be the first animal to go to the lion? They all looked at one another in silence.

Ijapa the tortoise was the first to speak. "My fellow animals, I am prepared to go to the lion; I am happy to be the first on the rota."

"You?" the animals chorused.

"Yes me. Why is everyone surprised?"

Everyone was quiet. They were relieved that the tortoise had volunteered to go first, but they were surprised because the tortoise was selfish and cunning and had never volunteered to do anything.

"Thank you for doing this, Ijapa. We promise to take care of your wife and children until it's their turn to go to the lion," said the owl.

"Well then, that's settled. Goodnight one and all," said Ijapa, and all the animals went to their houses.

The next day, the one-eyed lion waited patiently for his first meal but he didn't see any of the animals. *I'll wait another day; perhaps they are still deliberating on who will be the first to come to me,* he thought. On the second day, the lion waited all day, but still none of the animals came to the mountains. As he was about to start his terrible roar, he heard the voice of the tortoise.

"Greetings, great lion."

"Hello Ijapa. Are you my first meal?"

"Indeed I am, King of the Mountains."

"But why didn't you come yesterday? I waited all day."

"Your majesty, I did not mean to keep you waiting, but I had a terrible experience on my way here. I set out for the mountains, early yesterday morning but when I got to the great river that flows through Esho cave, a fierce creature stopped me; in fact, he threatened to kill me and I had to find another route through the forest to get here, hence my lateness."

"What fierce creature?"

"He looks exactly like you and he calls himself the king. He said…"

"…Nonsense! There's only one king and that is me!"

"Indeed, your majesty. I told him you are the only king and that you live on Mount Adawa, but he laughed scornfully and said if any other king existed, he will kill him."

The one-eyed lion stood up angrily. "In that case, take me to this imposter. I must show him who the real king is!" The tortoise pretended he was afraid. "Your majesty, this creature is evil. I saw him with my own two eyes and I believe he can tear anyone who comes near him to pieces. I don't think it is wise that you go after him."

"I said take me to him, and that is an order!"

"Okay, your majesty. Perhaps it is a good idea after all. If you don't kill him, none of us will be able to come to you, and you may eventually starve to death."

"Well, what are we waiting for Ijapa? Lead the way."

The tortoise turned around and led the one-eyed lion to the river by the cave. When they got there, the tortoise said,

"Your majesty, the creature is right there in the water, but please be careful." The lion was too angry to listen to the tortoise. He walked to the riverbank and looked down. To his amazement, he saw a creature staring at him; the creature looked exactly like him.

The angry lion shouted, "hey there, who are you?" He saw the creature's mouth move and he heard the same words he had spoken – "hey there, who are you?" "How dare you mimic me?" the lion shouted. Again, he heard an echo of his question.

He became angrier and leapt into the water, not knowing he'd been looking at his own reflection all along. He kicked and splashed, thinking he was fighting another lion. After a while, he became too tired to lift his paws or swim. Soon, his breath became shallow; he was weak because he hadn't eaten for a few days. Before long, the one-eyed lion sank to the bottom of the river.

The animals that had gathered to see what was happening gave a loud hurray and thanked Ijapa the tortoise for saving their lives. They danced and sang excitedly while the elephant trumpeted the praises of the tortoise through the village.

The Tortoise
and the
Three Brothers

Once upon a time, there were three orphans whose names were Otarun, Akope and Awekun. The brothers had reached such an age that it was time for them to decide what trade they might undertake. They decided to seek advice from Ijapa the tortoise, who had been their trusted guardian for many years. As soon as they arrived, Ijapa offered the brothers kola nuts and they all sat in his front yard under the acacia tree.

"Now, I am all ears," said Ijapa to his visitors. "What brings you here at this time of the day?"

Otarun was the first to speak. "Firstly, my brothers and I wish to say thank you for all you have done for us ever since our parents left this world to join our ancestors in the land beyond. Now we have each decided to learn a trade, and we would like you to advise us on this matter."

There was a moment of silence as the tortoise stared up at

the acacia tree, apparently lost in his own thoughts. The three brothers sat very still, all wondering what was going on in Ijapa's mind. Then the tortoise cleared his throat loudly and said, "I am happy that the three of you are thinking of learning a trade, but my advice to you is that you should join me in my business so that we can all work together."

The brothers looked at one another in amazement. Akope answered him. "We did not know that you have a business."

The tortoise laughed and said, "I do, child. However, my business involves much planning and scheming. I use more of my mind than my physical body. You may have noticed that I do not own a farm, neither do I buy and sell. I hold no position in the king's court, nor do I answer to any boss. Nevertheless, I eat well and I have everything I need."

Each of the brothers looked very shocked. This made Ijapa uncomfortable. "Why are you staring at me like that?" he asked. "I do not go around forcing people to part with their belongings! I am very cautious in my dealings with people. It is just that I always find a way of getting whatever I want, by hook or by crook."

There was another long silence. The brothers did not know what to say to Ijapa. Eventually, Otarun stood up and said, "We will be on our way now, but we will think about your proposal and give you an answer tomorrow before sunset."

The next day, Otarun was the only one who went to visit Ijapa. "My brothers and I have thought seriously about your offer," he announced, "and we want to thank you for thinking about us, but we cannot work for you. We are honest people and we would like honest trades. We want to work with our hands and we do not wish to take advantage of innocent people."

Ijapa's eyes narrowed in fury. "Is that what you have to say to me, after all I have done to support you since the death of your mother and father?" Otarun felt like a mouse that had just been trapped by a cat, but he stood his ground and answered, "I am sorry, but that is the way we feel."

"In that case," yelled Ijapa at the top of his voice, "you and your brothers have just made a vicious enemy!"

A few weeks later, the three brothers started learning their various new trades. They worked hard and applied themselves diligently to their tasks. They did as they were told; they listened to their bosses intently and soon became skilled and well respected among the villagers.

Otarun became the best archer the village had ever known, Akope provided the best palm wine the village had ever tasted, and Awekun became the best fisherman the village had ever seen; always catching the biggest haul of fish each morning.

But as the brothers' fame grew, so did Ijapa's jealousy; this fuelled Ijapa's plan to destroy them. He went to the palace one day and told the king that the trio had been boasting that they could perform some impossible stunts. The crafty tortoise feigned great sadness and said to the king, "I am concerned that people will start to believe what the brothers are saying. If this happens, I'm afraid our village will be in trouble!"

"How?" asked the king.

"Your highness, if people ask the orphans to perform these acts and they can't, do you realise what damage that will do to the reputation of our village? We will be known as the village of liars. People will say that we boast of things that are impossible. I think you should do something to stop this!"

The king became very angry after hearing Ijapa's speech. After all, a village was nothing without its good reputation, and it seemed that the orphan brothers were threatening the king's good name.

"Leave it with me, Ijapa," he said. "I know exactly what to do."

That same day, the king ordered the three brothers to his palace. As soon as they arrived, the king began to shout, "You are evil men. Before you destroy my kingdom I will destroy you! In exactly one week, I want you to return to my palace and prove to me that you are capable of the impossible feats that you have been boasting about all over the village."

The brothers attempted to protest their innocence, but the king held up his hand to silence them and bellowed with rage: "Otarun, you must shoot an arrow that will touch the sky! You, Akope, will climb the highest palm tree without a rope! And, Awekun, you must swim the length of the Odan River. I am giving you a chance to perform these stunts so that all of us might see if you are telling the truth. If you are not able to do as I have instructed, then you will be jailed for life!"

"Your highness, we did not claim such feats," Otarun protested, but the angry king was not ready to listen. Instead, he ordered his guards to escort the brothers from the palace and cast them out into the street.

The brothers were devastated. They sensed that Ijapa was the brains behind their predicament, but they did not know what to do. For many days they could not eat or sleep, yet they could find no solution to their problem. To make matters worse, they could not run away from the village because the king had assigned armed guards to watch over their every move. The brothers were not allowed to leave their house at any time.

On the day that the king told them to come to the palace, the three brothers were roused from their sleep by a strange sound. They opened the window to see a beautiful Bush Petronia perched on the tree outside their house. The bird was singing a solemn tune:

Song

Call:	*Omode meta nsere*
Response:	*Ere o, ere ayo*
Call:	*Okan l'ohun o ta'run*
Response:	*Ere o, ere ayo*
Call:	*Okan l'ohun o ga'gbon*
Response:	*Ere o, ere ayo*
Call:	*Okan l'ohun o we'kun*
Response:	*Ere o, ere ayo*
Call:	*O ta'run, O ga'gbon, O we'kun*
Response:	*Ere o ere ayo*

Translation

Call:	*Three children are playing*
Response:	*Playing, playing joyfully*
Call:	*One of them says he'll shoot his arrow to the sky*
Response:	*Playing, playing joyfully*
Call:	*One of them says he'll climb the palm tree without a rope*
Response:	*Playing, playing joyfully*

Call:	*One of them says he'll swim the length*
	and breadth of the great river
Response:	*Playing, playing joyfully*

The orphans were mesmerised by the melodious song. The verse, the gentle rhythm and the soothing lyrics were a sweet tune to their ears. Soon the bird flew away and the three brothers quickly stepped out of the house. The bird's song had revived their weary soul and they wanted to hear more. They wished the bird would come back and they waited under the tree. Unfortunately, there was no sign of the bird; however, they found three strange objects on the floor by the tree: a bow, a climbing rope and two golden armbands.

"How did these things get here?" Otarun asked. "They look quite… quite… unique." Just then, the brothers heard a chirping sound above them. "Those magical objects are gifts for you, but they are only visible to the three of you; no one else can see them." They looked up and saw that the bird was back on the tree.

"Thank you, kind bird; your beautiful song and precious gifts have given us hope," Akope said. "Make sure you use your gifts when you get to the king's palace today," said the bird, as he flew away. The brothers took their gifts and made their way to the palace where the king and his chiefs were seated in readiness for the feats to be performed. Ijapa also perched confidently beside the king, smiling wryly.

As the brothers entered the courtyard, a hush swept through the crowd and the king's words rang out loud and clear like the agogo bell. "Otarun, you claim to be able to shoot an arrow up to reach the sky; now perform this stunt of yours."

Otarun, who had his invisible bow in his left hand, took an arrow, placed it in the bow and shot it. Then he drew back and watched as the arrow soared high up into the sky and disappeared among the clouds above. The crowd erupted with joy, cheering and clapping for Otarun. The king, however, began to sweat profusely. He had never seen such a thing in his entire life.

Next, he called upon Akope to climb the tallest palm tree in the centre of the courtyard without a rope. Akope, who had already tied his magical rope around his waist and hooked it to a tree branch, began climbing the tree without a moment's hesitation. He scaled the tree as easily as any man might walk along a path, and he reached the top in no time at all. The crowd shouted out praise and clapped and cheered for Akope. By now, the king was growing quiet, and Ijapa too was looking uneasy. The king called upon Awekun to lead the group to the great Odan River.

Awekun was wearing his golden armbands, but they remained visible only to him and his brothers. He led the crowd to the river's edge and dived straight in. Once in the water he did not hesitate; he pulled with his arms, kicked with his legs and swam across the great river, darting to and fro with lightning speed. The drummers began to play their drums, while the people cheered and clapped.

The villagers hoisted the brothers up onto their shoulders and carried them back to the palace. Ijapa knew his end had come, so he tried to escape by sneaking through the assembled crowd as quickly as his sluggish little legs would carry him. But just as Ijapa was sure of his escape, one of the king's guards spotted him and cried out, "Not so fast, you mischievous old devil! Where do you think you're going?" The guard hoisted Ijapa up and carried him back into the palace.

The king called the orphan brothers to sit beside him on his throne as he addressed the people of the village. "I want to apologise to these brave young men," he announced. "I am sorry for falsely accusing them of being deceitful, and I apologise for the pain that I might have caused them." He turned to the three brothers and added, "I would like to honour you today by inviting you to be my chiefs."

The crowd erupted into more clapping, cheering and drumming as the brothers accepted the king's generous offer. The king turned to the tortoise and said, "As for you, Ijapa, you will be locked up in prison to serve the sentence you wished would be served upon these three brave brothers." The villagers all approved of the king's judgment and Ijapa was led away by the royal guards.

And as you can imagine, the three brothers lived happily ever after.

The Singing Drum

Once upon a time, there was a boy called Atilola. His parents loved him dearly because he was their only child and they made sure he had everything he wanted. They treated him like a delicate egg and would not allow anyone to reprimand him, even when he behaved badly. Because of this, Atilola found it difficult to do as he was told.

One day, during the rainy season, Atilola, who was ten years old at the time, told his mother that he was going outside to play with his friends.

"Stay in the neighbourhood and do not wander off into the valley; the sky is heralding rain," warned his mother, but as usual, Atilola ignored his mother's advice and ran off to find his friends.

"Let's go and look for honey in the beehive in Oyin valley," Atilola said to his friends once they had gathered together at the edge of the village. The boys agreed, and so they all set off on the four-mile journey in search of honey. As the boys approached Oyin, they noticed that the sky was beginning to turn grey. The first thunderclap made Atilola's friends panic.

39

One boy stepped forward and said, "we should get back to our homes before the rain comes." This was sensible advice and all the other boys, except Atilola, agreed to return home immediately.

"Not me!" yelled Atilola. "I have come here to find honey and I will not leave until I find some."

"But how can you find honey in the rain?" asked another boy.

"If I cannot find honey in the rain, then I will stay right here until it stops raining!" And just as the words left Atilola's mouth, tiny drops of rain began to fall from the sky, tickling the boys' bare backs. The other boys scampered off in the direction of the village leaving Atilola to hunt for the honey alone. Soon the little drops of rain formed a puddle and Atilola jumped around in it, splashing and dancing and waving his arms.

Some of the farmers returning from the fields saw Atilola dancing in the puddle and told him to go home, but the boy would not listen; instead, he wrinkled up his nose, stuck out his tongue and continued to dance in the puddle as the rain grew heavier and heavier.

As the sky continued to empty its contents in sheets and buckets, the heavy downpour flooded the entire valley in no time at all. Atilola couldn't find a place to hide. He looked around until eventually he saw an Odan tree and hurried towards it. Just as he was about to climb it, he slipped and fell into the water and the floods quickly engulfed him. As the waters carried Atilola down through the valley towards the big river, he screamed and howled in fear of his life, but there was nobody around to hear the frightened boy.

He tried to reach out and grab hold of anything that might

keep him afloat: twigs, logs, poles, but it was no use, he could not get a proper grip because he was moving too fast.

Then he saw a house in the distance and decided to scream at the top of his voice, hoping to gain the attention of those inside.

"Help!" he cried. "Please help me!"

Ijapa, the tortoise, heard the noise and opened his window to see what was happening. He was shocked to see a boy struggling to swim against the flood, so he hurried out of his house to help. He took a long pole from the shed in his front yard and stretched it out across the water towards the boy.

"Quick, grab a hold!" yelled Ijapa.

Atilola reached out for the pole and grabbed it with both hands, holding on tightly as Ijapa pulled him to safety. As soon as the boy was out of the water, Ijapa took him into the house, built a fire and served soup to warm him up. However, Ijapa was not generous by nature; all the time he was busy deciding what he might gain from the unsuspecting child.

This question was quickly answered after Atilola had drained his bowl of soup and curled up on a mat in a corner of the room. Before he drifted off to sleep, he began to sing in the most beautiful voice Ijapa had ever heard. It was a lullaby that his mother used to sing to him when he was a little boy.

Song:

Call:	*Ojo maa ro ojo maa ro; itura lo je*
Response:	*Ojo maa ro ojo maa ro; itura lo je*
Call:	*Eweko o yo boo ba ro*
Response:	*Eweko o yo*

41

Call:	*Agbado o yo boo ba ro*
Response:	*Agbado o yo*
Call:	*Emi o le leran lara boo ro*
Response:	*Emi o ni yo kun*
Call:	*Ojo maa ro ojo maa ro itura lo je*
Response:	*Ojo maa ro ojo maa ro itura lo je*

Translation

Call:	*Rain please fall; you are refreshing*
Response:	*Rain please fall; you are refreshing*
Call:	*Plants can't grow if you don't fall*
Response:	*Plants can't grow*
Call:	*Corn can't grow if you don't fall*
Response:	*Corn can't grow*
Call:	*I won't be healthy if you don't fall*
Response:	*I won't be healthy*
Call:	*Rain please fall; you are refreshing*
Response:	*Rain please fall; you are refreshing*

You can listen to or download the song from:
www.storytellerabi.bandcamp.com

Ijapa was mesmerised by the song, and as he swayed to the enchanting rhythm, a mischievous plan came into his mind. He waited until the boy was fast asleep, then crept out of the house to his backyard, where he began to carve a big wooden drum.

He worked throughout the night until his task was complete, and when Atilola awoke the next morning, Ijapa asked him to hop inside the drum.

"Why do you want me to get inside the drum?" asked Atilola.

The tortoise smiled innocently and told him that he simply wanted to test the drum's sound. "It is not such a huge favour to ask, given that I saved you from the floods, is it?" Atilola had to agree that he owed the tortoise a great debt for saving his life, and so he climbed inside the drum and the tortoise covered it over with stretched hide. He had already created small holes on the side of the wood so that the boy could breathe.

Once Atilola was hidden inside, Ijapa instructed him to sing the song 'Ojo maa ro' each time he hit the drum with a stick.

* * * *

Atilola's parents had been waiting anxiously for their son to return home. He had been gone all night and his mother was beside herself with worry. After the flood had subsided, both parents went into the valley in search of their son, but they could not find him anywhere. Eventually, they went to the palace to report Atilola missing. When the king heard the distressing news, he sent his servants to search the entire village and its environs. They too could not find the boy and eventually the search was abandoned.

Ijapa was unaware of all the commotion as he stood in the village square and shouted out to passers-by: "Come and listen to my singing drum! It is truly the most beautiful thing you will ever hear."

Many people gathered to witness the spectacle, and each time the tortoise banged on the drum with his stick, Atilola sang from within. All those who listened were enthralled by his beautiful voice. Many were so captivated by the singing drum that they threw their caps and headgear to the floor and danced until they could dance no more. Nobody could see the boy trapped inside; they all thought that it was a magical drum and so they gave the crafty tortoise a great deal of money for such entertainment. Word soon spread throughout the entire neighbourhood and everyone came to see Ijapa and his singing drum.

The following day, Ijapa was invited to the palace, as the king was also eager to listen to the magical singing drum. Ijapa was pleasantly surprised to see many people in the palace courtyard. The king had invited the entire village for the great entertainment, and there was not a single space left where one might sit.

The tortoise gained a great deal of confidence from the crowd and insisted that he be paid in gold before he played his drum. The king had never heard of such a request, but as he was so excited to hear the drum, he handed over a bag of gold and commanded the tortoise to begin.

Beaming with delight, Ijapa quickly banged on his drum, and again the beautiful voice began to sing the song 'Ojo maa ro'.

Call:	*Ojo maa ro ojo maa ro; itura lo je*
Response:	*Ojo maa ro ojo maa ro; itura lo je*
Call:	*Eweko o yo boo ba ro*
Response:	*Eweko o yo*

Call:	*Agbado o yo boo ba ro*
Response:	*Agbado o yo*
Call:	*Emi o le leran lara boo ro*
Response:	*Emi o ni yo kun*
Call:	*Ojo maa ro ojo maa ro itura lo je*
Response:	*Ojo maa ro ojo maa ro itura lo je*

The king, the chiefs and everyone in the palace courtyard immediately got up to dance. Despite such merriment and dancing, the king noticed a woman sitting in a corner. She was crying uncontrollably while her husband tried in vain to console her. The king stopped the entertainment immediately and ordered the couple to be brought before him. He was furious because it was taboo for anyone to cry in the presence of a monarch.

The woman bowed before the king and told him that Ijapa's drum was not magical at all; it was her son, Atilola, who was singing inside it, she was certain. "No mother could bear the thought of her only son being held prisoner in such a manner," she sobbed.

The king commanded his guards to tear off the hide from the top of the drum so that they might all see what was inside. When the hide was finally removed, Atilola slowly stepped out of the drum, blinking against the bright sun but grateful to be free at last.

When Atilola saw his parents, he ran to hug them, with tears of joy in his eyes. The entire palace erupted into a terrible commotion, as many people were shocked that Ijapa would deceive them in such a way.

The king ordered his guards to lock Ijapa up in jail, but the crafty tortoise was quick to point out to the king that the flood would have killed the boy had he not rescued him from the waters by pulling him to safety.

The king thought long and hard about Ijapa's defence and eventually decided to set the tortoise free, but the wise king warned against such tricks in the future, and he also took back his bag of gold for good measure.

As for Atilola, he decided that it was wiser to listen to his mother more often, and not to behave like such a spoilt child. And so it was that Atilola and his parents lived happily ever after.

THE TORTOISE, THE ELEPHANT AND THE HIPPOPOTAMUS

Once upon a time, Ijapa the tortoise had two great friends: the elephant and the hippopotamus. Everyday, these friends enjoyed playing together by the river at sunset. They played games, told stories and sang late into the night. Ijapa loved his two mighty friends dearly, but he wasn't happy that they made fun of him every time they played 'catch the ball'.

"Tell the slow coach to hurry up and fetch the ball," the hippopotamus would say to the elephant and the elephant would fall about laughing at the tortoise's stumpy legs. Ijapa did not tell his friends that their banter was annoying; instead, he decided to teach them a lesson.

One day, the three friends were playing by the beach and it was Ijapa's turn to fetch the large orange ball. The hippopotamus called out, "hey, Ijapa, I think we need to give those stumps of yours a stretch so you can move faster!" The elephant first giggled and then began to guffaw so much that he became breathless.

Ijapa turned around to face his friends and said, "I've had enough of your rudeness; I may be small and stout, but I can beat you hands down in a rope-pulling game!"

"What?" said the elephant. He couldn't believe his ears.

"You must be joking," the hippopotamus sniggered.

"No, I'm not joking; let's meet here tomorrow morning and I'll bring a rope. All you need to do is get yourselves ready for the contest of your life, and make sure you have a good night's rest because of the hard work that you'll be doing tomorrow."

The following morning, Ijapa headed for the elephant's house and told him to come out to a clearing. He gave him one end of the long rope and told him to hold on to it until he heard the djembe drum signalling the start of the contest.

"Don't leave this place; just pull the rope and I will be at the other end pulling," he said to the mighty elephant.

"Watch your back, my friend," the elephant giggled. "I will throw you about with this rope and you may land on your shell."

Ijapa ignored him and headed for the river, where the hippopotamus was waiting. He gave him the other end of the rope and told him to hold on to it until he heard the djembe drum.

"You must pull very hard, my friend," he said to the hippopotamus, "or you'll find yourself hurled out of the river. I will be at the other end pulling."

"Are you sure you don't want to change your mind?" the

hippopotamus jibed. "One tiny pull from me and you may end up in your grave."

Ijapa pretended he did not hear his friend's comment. He made his way to the middle of the forest, where he had already placed a drum, and began to play a tune on his djembe:

Dun godo dun go
Dun godo dun go

The elephant and hippopotamus recognised the sound as the sign for the contest to begin, and they began to pull. Ijapa climbed up a tree so he could see both animals battle with the rope. Initially, they pulled leisurely, thinking that the contest would end within seconds, but they soon realised it was no child's play, so they intensified their efforts and pulled as though their lives depended on it.

By mid-afternoon, they had become so exhausted that they were ready to give up. Ijapa saw the elephant and the hippopotamus coming to look for him and quickly came down from the tree to where the centre of the rope was. He took a knife, cut the rope into two, and held the ends in each hand.

When his exhausted friends saw him, they were flabbergasted. They saw Ijapa holding the two ends of the rope and felt humiliated; they thought Ijapa had been pulling both of them. Neither of them knew that Ijapa had tricked them and that they had been pulling each other.

"Shall we do this again tomorrow?" Ijapa asked gleefully.

"No!" the elephant yelled. "Ijapa, you are indeed a powerful animal… despite your size." Ijapa turned to the hippopotamus. "And what have you to say?" he asked.

"I agree with the elephant, you definitely have supernatural strength. I still can't get my head round the fact that you've been pulling me with just one hand!"

"And me," the elephant moaned. "He's been pulling me with one hand too."

Ijapa smiled wryly. "If both of you say you've had enough, I won't argue with you," he said as he turned to leave. "I'll take this rope home and you can go and rest now."

"Can we keep this between us? Please don't let the other animals know about our rope contest," the hippopotamus called out to the tortoise. "I'll think about it", the tortoise replied. He knew that from that day on, his friends would treat him with respect. He was right. The elephant and the hippopotamus never made fun of Ijapa the tortoise again.

And so it was that the three friends continued to play together happily ever after.

THE HUNTER,
THE ALIENS AND
THE TORTOISE

Many years ago, there lived a highly skilled hunter who everyone in the village and neighbouring towns respected. He had learnt his skill from his grandfather and had been hunting since he was a teenager. Unfortunately, this hunter was very poor because even though he was hardworking, he gave the animals that he hunted to his friends and neighbours, instead of selling them to make money.

Soon there were no animals left in the forest because he had killed them all. So the man decided to start hunting birds. One day, he took his gear and went to work. He roamed the forest from morning until evening, but couldn't find a single bird. Later, just before sunset, he heard some sparrows singing. He crept under a tree and shot at them, and one of the sparrows tumbled down. "At last," he sighed as he picked up the wounded bird.

The hunter was very tired because he'd been wandering around the forest all day, so he decided to take a nap under a tree. When he woke up, he couldn't find the bird; it had flown away. The hunter's gun had barely scraped its wings. "Back to square one," he muttered as he set out to find another bird. Although it was late evening, the hunter wasn't ready to give up. *I must hunt a little more or my efforts will be in vain*, he thought.

Soon, it was dark, and after wandering around the forest for a long time, he lost his way. He came to a narrow path and followed it to see where it would lead; to his disappointment, the path did not lead him out of the forest but to a huge baobab tree in an open space. Around the tree were some strange creatures; they seemed to be having a meeting. These aliens were the most unusual and bizarre creatures the hunter had ever seen, even though he was a reputable hunter who had seen nearly every type of strange animal. The aliens had no whole form; they had huge heads, with one eye in the middle of their faces, crooked legs, grotesque looking thighs and huge hairy ears. Suddenly, they turned and fixed their single squinted eyes on the hunter, ready to pounce on him.

The hunter begged and assured them that he had not intentionally gate-crashed their meeting, and explained how he was lost and couldn't find his way out of the forest. A large head moved towards the hunter; he was the leader of the clan.

"Alien from the land of the whole," he bellowed in a deep sonorous voice, "what is your story? We have not had a visit from your people for many centuries; we even believed you were extinct. How did you get here? Our territory is far away from your forest."

The hunter narrated his story. He told them how skilled he

was, the reason for his poverty and how he had got lost in the forest. "In fact, I am about to give up on life," the hunter lamented when he had finished his story of woe.

"Hmmm…" the leader sighed. "Do you have any other skills? It is obvious that you cannot continue hunting."

"I once worked as a palm wine tapper, but I haven't done that in many years," the hunter replied. The aliens' eyes lit up. "Palm wine," they echoed. The leader turned to the other aliens and whispered something to them. They all nodded excitedly and he turned to the hunter.

"We would like to help you. If you are able to tap palm wine, we would be happy to buy it for good money."

The hunter didn't waste time to think it through. He agreed there and then to be a regular supplier of palm wine to the aliens. He thanked them and asked that they show him the way out of the forest. He promised to come back in three days with the first gourd of palm wine.

"When you bring the palm wine, pour it into the tank behind that acacia tree," said the leader, pointing to a tree beyond the clearing. "You will find your money under the tank. After you've poured the wine, take your money and go away; you must never look back to see us drinking; do you understand?"

"Yes, I do," the hunter assured him and went on his way. He could hardly believe his good luck. The following day, he went to the market to buy a climbing rope and a couple of large gourds. He then went out to find some mature palm trees and began his new career as a wine tapper.

On the third day, he made his way to the aliens' abode to supply them with palm wine. When he got there he began to sing:

Song:

Call:	*Ara orun, ara orun*
Response:	*Inomba tere, gun gun tere, Inomba*
Call:	*Tani npe ara orun?*
Response:	*Inomba tere, gun gun tere, Inomba*
Call:	*Emi ademu ni*
Response:	*Inomba tere, gun gun tere, Inomba*
Call:	*Elo le'mu re?*
Response:	*Inomba tere, gun gun tere, Inomba*
Call:	*Keregbe kan egbaa*
Response:	*Inomba tere, gun gun tere, Inomba*
Call:	*Gbe'mu sile, ko maa lo*
Response:	*Inomba tere gun gun tere, Inomba*

Translation

Call:	*Aliens, oh aliens*
Response:	*Inomba tere, gun gun tere, Inomba*
Call:	*Who is calling the aliens?*
Response:	*Inomba tere, gun gun tere, Inomba*
Call:	*It's me, the palm wine tapper*
Response:	*Inomba tere, gun gun tere, Inomba*
Call:	*How much is your palm wine?*
Response:	*Inomba tere, gun gun tere, Inomba*
Call:	*Ten shillings per gourd*
Response:	*Inomba tere, gun gun tere, Inomba*
Call:	*Pour the palm wine and go on your way*

*Inomba tere, gun gun tere is an onomatopoeic phrase or chorus that comes after each dialogue.

The hunter found his payment under the tank, took it and quickly left the forest without looking back. He continued supplying wine to the aliens and soon became rich. The aliens bought all his wine and he had a steady income.

A few months later, the hunter became ill. There was an outbreak of guinea worm disease in his village and his legs were infected. He was bedridden for three months and couldn't supply the aliens with their palm wine. One day, he called his friend Ijapa the tortoise, and asked him to take gourds of wine to the aliens until he was back on his feet. The tortoise agreed to do the job and the hunter told him the protocol. He warned him never to look back at the aliens and to quickly leave the forest once he'd collected the money.

The tortoise started supplying the aliens palm wine and he didn't look back at them. However, on his fourth run, he decided to hide behind a tree to watch the strange creatures as they drank.

Soon, the aliens came out one after the other, led by their leader. They threw themselves into the tank and frantically swam around in the wine, in a chaotic manner, until the tank was empty and each of them began to burp loudly. The tortoise couldn't control himself any longer. He began to laugh very loudly, shouting, "Is this what forest aliens look like? Look at those ugly heads and oh those strange looking hairy ears. See how they are gulping down palm wine, the greedy lot!"

The aliens were shocked. "The hunter has betrayed us," shouted the leader. "This intruder must pay for his rudeness; search for the fool!" They looked everywhere and found Ijapa hiding behind a tree. Just as they were about to grab him, he jumped into a hole underneath it. The aliens began to dig around, but initially they couldn't catch Ijapa. Soon, they found his feet and pulled them, but the cunning tortoise laughed and said, "silly aliens, you're merely pulling at the root of the tree". They quickly let go and pulled the root of the tree, and the tortoise screamed: "Help, that's my leg you're pulling; leave me alone!" Then the aliens pulled harder.

Thus, the tortoise continued to trick the aliens. Each time they caught his legs, he would yell that it was the root of the tree, and when they pulled the root of the tree, he would scream that it was his legs. This continued throughout the afternoon, and the aliens became very tired. They decided to go back to their homes, but vowed that whenever the hunter came back, they would kill him.

Meanwhile, in the village, the hunter was waiting impatiently for Ijapa because he was unusually late. He feared the tortoise was up to no good.

"Where have you been?" he asked as soon as the tortoise came in with the empty gourd.

"I... I... was stopped by bandits and they took all the palm wine," he lied. The hunter scratched his head uneasily; he didn't believe the tortoise, but he didn't say anything. A few weeks later, he was back on his feet and he took palm wine to the aliens. When he got to the forest, he began to sing:

Call:	*Ara orun, ara orun*
Response:	*Inomba tere, gun gun tere, Inomba*
Call:	*Tani npe ara orun?*
Response:	*Inomba tere, gun gun tere, Inomba*
Call:	*Emi ademu ni*
Response:	*Inomba tere, gun gun tere, Inomba*

Call:	*Elo le'mu re?*
Response:	*Inomba tere, gun gun tere, Inomba*
Call:	*Keregbe kan egbaa*
Response:	*Inomba tere, gun gun tere, Inomba*
Call:	*Gbe'mu sile ko maa lo*
Response:	*Inomba tere, gun gun tere, Inomba*

The hunter noticed the sourness in the voices of the aliens as they spoke to him. Before he knew it, they surrounded him and began to attack. They did not give the hunter a chance to explain himself; they were determined to kill him, but the hunter was a good fighter. He was a skilled hunter who had been trained to protect himself against the attacks of deadly beasts. His training came in handy as he defended himself.

It was a deadly battle. They fought from morning until night, but the aliens could not overpower the hunter. The leader beckoned to the other aliens, who had started to sway unsteadily. "Listen, fellows, I've had enough of this; tell the others to stop fighting the hunter and let's call a truce."

Everyone was wounded. The leader himself was bruised and the hunter was limping. When the fighting stopped, he asked the hunter why he had sent Ijapa to make fun of them.

The hunter was shocked to hear what Ijapa had done and he told the aliens about his illness. "I thought it would be good to find someone to supply you with palm wine because I was bedridden for such a long time. I didn't know Ijapa would betray me this way, I am very sorry."

The aliens accepted his apology. "Would you like to continue to supply us with palm wine?" Head asked.

"Yes, I would like that very much," the hunter replied.

"In that case, the business is still yours." The other aliens nodded in agreement, and the hunter thanked everyone.

As the hunter picked up his gourd, the leader whispered in his ear, "You must choose your friends wisely. All lizards crawl on their bellies, but you may never know the ones that have belly ache."

"Lizards... belly ache?" the hunter muttered.

Head laughed at the hunter. "You humans have lost touch with proverbs. What I mean is, it is impossible to read people's minds; therefore, you may never know who is a true friend."

The hunter thanked the aliens and went on his way. He continued to take fresh palm wine to his friends. Soon he became the richest palm wine tapper in the village, and he lived happily ever after.

THE TORTOISE
AND THE EAGLE

Once upon a time, there were two unusual friends: Ijapa the tortoise and Awodi the eagle. These two friends lived in different worlds; the eagle's home was in the great sky and the tortoise lived in the deep forest. Nevertheless, their friendship continued to blossom and this convinced the other animals that distance should never be a barrier to friendship.

Ijapa's family always looked forward to the visit of Awodi, and they took good care of him every time he came down to see them. However, Awodi took his friend's hospitality for granted. He never invited Ijapa or his family to his own house, and every time he visited Ijapa, ate his food and enjoyed his company, he would make fun of him as he flew back home. "Hee hee hee, I can eat Ijapa's food but he can never come to my pretty penthouse," he would say. Then, in a high-pitched note, he would start to sing:

Song:

Call: *Ko s'oloko loko*
Response: *Eye bere maa j'eka, eye*

Translation

Call:	*The farmer is away*
Response:	*Come down dear bird, and eat up all his crops*

Soon, the entire forest knew about the selfish eagle and his chants. One day, Opolo the frog, who did not like the eagle because he always swooped down to carry one of his froglets home for supper, went to see Ijapa. "My friend, do you realise that Awodi is taking you for granted?"

Ijapa scratched his head uneasily before answering, "what do you mean?'"

"Well, did you know that every time he visits, he makes fun of you on his way back to his house and he says, 'Hee hee hee, I can eat Ijapa's food but he can never come to my pretty penthouse?' To add insult to injury, he mocks you with a song."

"What song?" Ijapa asked.

Opolo cleared his throat and began to sing:

Call:	*Ko s'oloko loko*
Response:	*Eye bere maa j'eka, eye*

Ijapa was furious, but he controlled his anger. "Thank you, Opolo", I appreciate your concern for me and I'll do something about it."

When the eagle visited the next time, Ijapa said to him. "Awodi, every time you come here, you do not take food back to your family; that's not good. Next time you visit, bring a large container so that we can send them food."

Awodi was excited. "Thanks my friend, I'll do just that."
After eating, he bade Ijapa and his family goodbye, and sang
his mocking song as he flew away.

On his next visit, Awodi brought a large gourd. Yanibo,
Ijapa's wife, welcomed him as he arrived.

"Where's Ijapa?" Awodi asked.

"He's gone to visit his relatives and won't be back for a few
days. He told me to fill your container with food for your
family. Sit down here and eat what we've prepared for you, I'll
be back soon." Ijapa's wife took the gourd out to the kitchen
and Ijapa, who was hiding in the backyard, crept inside it
quietly. His wife covered him with fresh food and took the
gourd back to Awodi, who had finished eating and was about
to set out.

"Thank you so much; give my love to your husband when
he returns," said the eagle, and he flew away laughing and
singing as usual. The tortoise, who was hiding in the gourd,
could hear his chant: "Hee hee hee, I can eat Ijapa's food but
he can never come to my pretty penthouse". Then Awodi
began to sing:

Call: *Ko s'oloko loko*
Response: *Eye bere maa j'eka, eye*

The tortoise almost choked with anger, but he held back from
screaming at the eagle. When Awodi arrived home, he
emptied out the container onto his kitchen floor and Ijapa
crawled out and said, "my dear friend, I thought it would be
nice to visit your pretty penthouse, as you have always enjoyed

67

my hospitality."

Awodi shouted at him angrily, "you fool, I'll peck all the flesh off your bone and teach you not to trick the mighty eagle." He began to peck at Ijapa's hard shell but he couldn't continue because his beak hurt so much that he feared he might lose his treasured nib.

The tortoise was taken aback. "Is this what you call friendship, you selfish bird? Take me back to the forest, I've had enough of you!"

"Forest, what forest?" Awodi yelled at Ijapa. "I'll take you all right, but I will throw you to the ground and that hard shell of yours will no longer serve you."

"You will do no such thing," Ijapa yelled as he bit Awodi's leg and would not let go.

"Leave my leg alone, nasty creature!"

"Not until you deliver me safe and sound to my family," the tortoise muttered, whilst holding firmly to the eagle's leg. The eagle, by now, was in so much pain that he quickly flew out of his house. He tried to shake Ijapa off his leg as he descended, but couldn't, so he continued to plunge through the floating clouds until he set Ijapa down safely in his home.

The tortoise was glad to be back with his family. He called out to Awodi, "I'm sorry our friendship has to end this way, but you are no longer welcome in my home."

THE TORTOISE
AND THE PIG

Once upon a time, in Ijapa's village, the animals prepared for the planting season. Everyone was busy during the day and they sometimes worked late into the night.

However, while the other animals were busy planting their seeds in the farm, Ijapa lazed around under the acacia tree in his front yard and watched the lizards chasing insects.

Many months passed and all the animals looked after their crops and waited patiently for them to grow. Soon, it was harvest and everyone was excited. Harvest season was usually a time of merrymaking; it was also a time when the farmers showed off their produce.

On the day of the harvest celebration, all the farmers gathered in the village square and brought their crops for blessing. They had worked very hard and were grateful for what the land had yielded. The whole square was bursting with fruits and vegetables of all kinds: mango, banana, papaya, orange, carrot, potato, yam, cucumber, and much more.

Ijapa woke up earlier than usual and made his way to the square. The pleasant smell of ripe fruits hit his nose as he arrived; he had been looking forward to the ceremony for months. When everyone had arrived, the lion called the owl to open the ceremony with a short thanksgiving.

The owl cleared his throat and said:

"We give thanks for the ploughing, sowing and reaping.
We give thanks for the silent growth while we sleep.
We give thanks for the thunderous rain.
And now we give thanks for the bountiful harvest.
Amen."

All the animals clapped in jubilation and the lion declared the ceremony open with the rain song. The animals in the square erupted into singing:

Call:	*Ojo maa ro ojo maa ro; itura lo je*
Response:	*Ojo maa ro ojo maa ro; itura lo je*
Call:	*Eweko o yo boo ba ro*
Response:	*Eweko o yo*
Call:	*Agbado o yo boo ba ro*
Response:	*Agbado o yo*
Call:	*Emi o le leran lara boo ro*
Response:	*Emi o ni yo kun*
Call:	*Ojo maa ro ojo maa ro itura lo je*
Response:	*Ojo maa ro ojo maa ro itura lo je*

Translation

Call:	*Rain please fall; you are refreshing*
Response:	*Rain please fall; you are refreshing*
Call:	*Plants can't grow if you don't fall*
Response:	*Plants can't grow*
Call:	*Corn can't grow if you don't fall*
Response:	*Corn can't grow*
Call:	*I won't be healthy if you don't fall*
Response:	*I won't be healthy*
Call:	*Rain please fall; you are refreshing*
Response:	*Rain please fall; you are refreshing*

**You can listen to or download the song from:
www.storytellerabi.bandcamp.com**

The dogs and monkeys began to play joyful tunes on the djembes, while the other animals danced and sang loudly.

Soon it was time for them to show off their crops. The rains had been steady throughout, so the yams and cassavas looked healthy. Elede, the pig, who lived next door to Ijapa, had the biggest yam that year; his produce was so enormous that he had to get the elephant to help him move it. After the crops show, the animals sat down to enjoy a sumptuous dinner.

The following morning, Ijapa went round to see his neighbour the pig, pretending that he wanted to wish him well for winning the 'best farmer of the year' competition. The award was given to Elede at the harvest celebration.

"Good morning, my friend, congratulations on your achievement!"

"Thanks for your well wishes," Elede grunted. "What brings you to my sty so early in the morning?"

"Oh, just to say well done. I was really proud of you when the announcement was made yesterday. I said to myself, there goes my hard-working neighbour."

"Thank you, but I must get on now. I need to sell my crops at the market."

"Indeed, indeed, but, erm… before you go, could you do me a favour?"

"Certainly, if it is something I can do."

"I'm very sure you can," the cunning tortoise replied. "You see, my wife's family is visiting us tonight and I must feed them, but I don't have any food in the house. I just want to buy one of your yams."

"Of course you can," the pig squealed in delight. "I'm not doing you a favour; you are helping me. You are buying my yam."

"Well, the reason I said favour is because I can only buy it on credit. I am expecting some money from my debtors and I will pay you back next week." The pig was hesitant to sell his yam on credit to Ijapa, especially because of his bad reputation. He had never paid back anything he owed. Ijapa noticed Elede's hesitancy and quickly added, "I am happy to pay extra for your yam, just name your price."

The pig thought long and hard. He was a kind animal, who always wanted to help, so he decided to sell a tuber of yam to the tortoise. "I will come to your house next week to collect my money," he said to the tortoise.

Seven days later, the pig went to visit Ijapa as agreed, but he met the tortoise in his backyard crying and wearing a black cloth.

"What's the matter, Ijapa?"

The tortoise heaved a sigh and bowed his head. "It's my mother in-law, she died this morning."

"I am so sorry, my friend. I'll come back on another day," said the pig, and he left Ijapa's house. Elede made several visits to Ijapa's house but the tortoise always had one excuse or another for not paying the money he owed. One day, the pig threatened that if Ijapa did not pay him when next he came, he would take him to the king. He stomped his feet angrily as he left the tortoise, but he promised to come back the following day.

Later that evening, Ijapa said to his wife, Yanibo, "listen my dear, you know we don't have any money to pay Elede, and he's coming back tomorrow. Here's what we'll do. When he arrives, I will draw my head and limbs into my shell and you must turn me over so that I lie on my back. Then place some pepper on my belly and pretend you're grinding it."

Just before sunrise the following day, Ijapa and his wife heard the pig coming into their front yard. The tortoise drew his limbs and head into his shell and Yanibo quickly turned him over and placed a large pepper on his belly.

"Greetings," the pig called from outside.

"Please come in; I'm grinding pepper in the backyard," Yanibo replied.

"Where is your husband?" the pig asked.

"He's gone out to see …"

Elede would not listen to another word. He walked up to Yanibo, snatched the grinding mill, not knowing it was Ijapa, and hurled it over the fence into the bush behind the house.

"Tell your husband that I will be back in a few hours, and he had better have my money ready", he yelled as he stormed out of the house. A few hours later, Elede went back to Ijapa's house.

"Aha, the pig I wanted to see," Ijapa said cheerily. "I have your money ready, my friend, please come and sit down while I fetch it for you."

"I'm okay standing, just give me my money," said the pig.

Ijapa called to his wife. "Yanibo, please bring your grinding stone; I hid Elede's money in it."

"Well, Elede threw it into the bush in anger, when I told him you had gone out."

The tortoise slowly turned to the pig. "Did you really throw my wife's grinding stone away?" Ijapa asked, feigning anger.

"I'm sorry, I'll go and fetch it right away," said the pig. He quickly made his way to the bush behind Ijapa's house and began to search frantically, but he couldn't find the grinding stone. He dug through the dry leaves, twigs and dirt with his snout, but the stone was nowhere to be found.

Today, you can still see Elede the pig, rooting in the dirt, trying to find Yanibo's grinding stone.

How the Tortoise Became Bald

In the beginning, Ijapa the tortoise had hair, and lots of it. His locks were long, thick and flowing, but one day Ijapa lost every strand because of his greed. This is how it happened:

Many years ago, Ijapa's friend, Aja the dog, invited him to his new puppy's naming ceremony. Ijapa was excited because he knew that Aja's wife was a brilliant cook; she always made delicious meals and served generous sizes and even gave takeaways. On the day of the ceremony, Ijapa made his way to his friend's house to celebrate with him and eat good food. It was a hot and humid Saturday morning and the sun shone brightly in the sky. Ijapa wore his special Yoruba attire: a dashiki with matching trousers and a matching cap. He had his locks neatly tucked into the cap and he was sweating profusely.

He walked down the red dust path that led to Aja's house, and soon saw it in the distance. A few yards from the house, Ijapa could smell the pleasant scent of delicious food. *Sniff, sniff*, he breathed deeply as the aroma of mouth-watering yam porridge, seasoned with smoked fish and spicy herbs, wafted towards him. Ijapa rubbed his protruding belly and smiled. "It is going to be a good day," he muttered and hastened his steps.

Ijapa was the first guest to arrive at his friend's house. He did not bring a gift for the new puppy, nor did he bring a gift for Aja's wife. He greeted the family hastily. "Congratulations, my friends, when is this ceremony going to start?"

"As soon as the elders arrive."

"Must you wait for the elders? You and your wife should just name the puppy and we can start eating."

"No, we have to follow tradition; this is our first puppy and the entire family is coming to bless him."

"Ah well, suit yourself", Ijapa replied.

Soon, Aja's family and friends arrived and gave him and his wife gifts and admired the beautiful new puppy. Then the head of Aja's clan rose up to start the ceremony.

"We are gathered here to name this new puppy, but we must first bless him," the elder announced. Ijapa was becoming restless. He could no longer wait for the food; the aroma pervaded the house and he was salivating. He crept out of the front room, where people were praying for the new puppy, and made his way to the backyard, looking for the kitchen.

Aja's wife and her friends had finished cooking and everyone had gone to the front room, so there was nobody in the backyard. Ijapa found the kitchen, and as he entered, his belly made a loud rumbling noise. There was a large cast iron pot in the corner of the room and Ijapa quickly took off the lid. He nearly fainted as the steam from the delicious yam porridge enveloped him. He grabbed a spoon and scooped some porridge into a bowl. He gobbled it down and cried, "Aha! That was the most delicious yam I've ever eaten."

However, the impatient tortoise wanted more; he started thinking of how he could smuggle some tasty porridge out of Aja's house, without him knowing.

"Nobody knows when that ceremony will finish; I need some good food in my belly and I need it now," he moaned.

Ijapa smiled as a thought came to his mind. He took off his cap and filled it with hot yam porridge. *That'll sit nicely on my head while I go and give Aja some lame excuse as to why I have to leave early*, he thought as he made his way to the dogs' front room.

Aja's guests were rejoicing when Ijapa arrived. The local storyteller was entertaining them with drumming and chants; everyone was happy for the new parents and they were singing:

Call:	*Omo o e npe dagba*
Response:	*Omo o e npe dagba*
Call:	*Kekere jojolo mo gbe temi*
Response:	*Omo o e npe dagba*
Call:	*B'omo mi dagba a s'ori ire*
Response:	*Omo o e npe dagba*

Translation

Call:	*Children grow up soon*
Response:	*Children grow up soon*
Call:	*I will tenderly nurture my child*
Response:	*Children grow up soon*
Call:	*When my child grows up she will be responsible*
Response:	*Children grow up soon*

You can listen to or download the song from:
www.storytellerabi.bandcamp.com

Aja and his wife were dancing in the centre of the room. Aja held his puppy proudly and moved with such gracefulness that everyone soon joined them and the merriment continued.

Meanwhile, Ijapa was becoming very restless because of the hot porridge in his cap. He quickly stepped out of the room but the host and guests noticed his strange behaviour. Aja followed Ijapa and called out to him. "My friend, where are you going? The party is just starting."

"Erm… um… I have to go; I don't feel too well."

Aja noticed something dripping from Ijapa's cap and he became suspicious. "Do you have a boil on your head? It looks like pus is coming out of it," Aja called out to the tortoise, who was scuttling out of the house. More guests were now coming outside to witness the drama.

The tortoise shouted: "No, I don't have a boil on my head, you go back to your guests and stop following me! I'll be fine."

Aja refused to go back; he knew Ijapa was up to no good.

83

He'd been missing from the ceremony for a while anyway and Aja had wondered where he was.

The tortoise was in so much pain that he began to yell, "my head is on fire," as he ran towards the brook. When he got there, he took his cap off, flung it into the river and dived into the cool water. The guests could see the yam porridge floating in the river. When he came out of the water, everyone gasped in disbelief. Ijapa's head was totally bald! The hot porridge had burned deeply into his scalp and he was scarred for life. From that day onwards, no hair grew on Ijapa's head again.

The incident had a devastating effect on the tortoise; he lost his appetite for cooked meals after that fateful day, and he decided that dark, leafy, green vegetables were more appetising.

THE TORTOISE
AND THE
GELADA BABOON

Once upon a time, there was a great famine in Gondar, the city where Ijapa the tortoise had immigrated to, when he was chased out of his hometown in Ibadan, for causing mayhem. The people of Gondar welcomed him and he enjoyed his stay there, but it seems the famine was about to devastate the land. Many animals were dying and Ijapa knew he had to move again. He heard that there was food on the ancient Simien Mountains, so he set out on the long journey to the North. He stopped in villages and towns on the way, to beg for food and shelter and after many weeks, he arrived at Simien late one night, when many of the animals had gone to sleep. Luckily for Ijapa, Amsalu the horse was still ploughing. He saw how tired Ijapa was and he gave him food and a place to sleep.

The next day, Ijapa was about to go and look for something to eat, when he saw Amsalu. He thanked him again for his hospitality and asked where he could find food.

"Listen, Ijapa, many animals have come to the mountains from various towns and villages because of the famine in the lowlands, but very soon, the vegetation here will dry up and we'll all starve to death."

"Oh dear!" cried the tortoise, who could not bear the thought of moving again.

"Don't be afraid, there's hope," Amsalu assured him. "I have just heard that some farmers are bringing seeds to Chenek market, but I can't go there right now; I need to plough my land. If you can bring some seeds from the market, I'll buy them from you and you will have money to buy food and take care of yourself." Although the tortoise was excited about the good news, he did not welcome the idea of travelling to Chenek.

"It is a very long journey for a small animal," said Amsalu, "and I know you don't like hard work, but think about the future. If we don't plant now, we'll all starve to death later."

"Why don't you ask Mulu? He moves very fast and…"

"Never! I can't tell him about this. He'll… he… Listen, let's just say you are the best person to get us seeds, Ijapa."

"Mulu won't eat the seeds, if that's what you're afraid of. Geladas only eat grass."

"That's where you're wrong. You don't live on these mountains, so you don't know them. If you ask a Gelada to choose between grass and seeds he will go for seeds."

"Alright, I'll go to the market," said the tortoise after a while.

"Great! I wish you a safe journey," said Amsalu.

The tortoise set out for the market that day and didn't return until the following evening. On his way back, he saw Mulu and tried to avoid him.

"Greetings, my friend," Mulu called. "What's in that sack of yours?"

Ijapa did not answer; he moved faster and tried to get away from the baboon, but Mulu, who hadn't eaten for a few days, took a sniff and smelled grass seeds. His stomach rumbled loudly. "Food at last!" he rejoiced and ran after the tortoise.

"My friend, can I have some of your seeds?" he asked, as he caught up with Ijapa.

"Umm… that wouldn't be possible; they are for the king."

"Why does the king need grass seeds?"

"I… I… I think he wants them for his new field," the tortoise lied.

"Well, the king will not miss a handful, will he?"

"Oh yes, he will. Every seed was counted by…"

"Look, I am really hungry and not in the mood for an argument or long conversation; all I want is a handful of seeds."

"Sorry, the answer is still NO!" Ijapa said emphatically.

"In that case, I WILL help myself," Mulu replied grimacing. He flipped his upper lip back and showed a set of long, ferocious teeth. The tortoise quickly dropped his sack and moved backwards.

Mulu grabbed the sack, dipped his hands into it and began to eat. Mmm… absolutely delicious! Where did you get these seeds from, Ijapa? Surely they are not from these mountains."

Ijapa was fuming with rage. "You are so greedy, Mulu, you asked for just a handful, but now you've eaten all my seeds. I have been travelling for many hours, just to get the sack back to the mountains. I am only a tiny animal, and a slow one at that, it wasn't easy for me to bring it here from the market!"

Mulu munched and munched until he couldn't eat a single seed more. Then he smacked his lips, turned around and walked away, leaving the tortoise with an empty sack. Ijapa was distraught.

A few months later, Mulu set out early one morning to visit his friends. On his way, he heard an ant calling out in pain, so he stopped to see what was happening. He saw a rat twiddling with the ant, who was already paralysed with fear, and threatening to eat him.

"Leave him alone!" Mulu shouted.

"Why? This is none of your business!"

"I make it my business when bullies like you torment innocent animals."

"You mean, like you tormented poor Ijapa when you ate up his seeds," the rat retorted. He threw the ant on the floor and ran away before Mulu could say another word.

"Thanks ever so much," the ant called out to Mulu. "One day I will repay you." Mulu laughed. "Ha ha ha! What's your name tiny ant?"

"My name is Leul; I am a prince."

"Ha! What can a tiny ant like you do for me?" Mulu sniggered.

On his way, Mulu saw the tortoise standing under a Juniper tree, braiding the hair of Amsalu the horse. Mulu was fascinated by the nimbleness and speed with which the tortoise created intricate designs on the horse's mane, and he stopped to watch.

"Greetings," said Mulu. "That is such a beautiful design;

who taught you to weave like that?" Ijapa pretended not to hear Mulu and continued to weave Amsalu's hair.

"I said, what an amazing skill you've got there, my friend; that hair looks splendid!"

"Thank you, Mulu," the tortoise replied. "I didn't realise you were watching me. You have got beautiful hair, too. There's no other animal on this mountain whose hair looks as amazing and sleek as yours. I've always wondered why you never asked me to braid your hair so you can show off your beauty."

"Thank you, but this is the first time I've seen you weave. I didn't know you had such a great skill. I'd like my hair braided too, if you don't mind."

"I don't mind at all. I'll soon finish weaving Amsalu's hair and you can be my next client, but you don't have to pay me anything; it is free of charge.

"Really?"

"Yes. Do you doubt my generosity?" Amsalu is not paying me anything for his braids. I'm just so bored today and I decided to make some animals happy."

"That's very kind of you, tortoise. I'll just wait here for my turn."

Soon, the tortoise finished weaving Amsalu's hair and he called Mulu to sit on the floor under the tree. The tortoise mounted a wooden stool and began to pull the Gelada's hair. "What a luxurious mane you've got here," he said. "It's very long; I will need to use some branches to keep them in sections so they don't get matted while I braid some rows."

With that, he came down from the stool and told Mulu to help him get on a branch so he could braid his hair. Ijapa told

Mulu to stand on the wooden stool, so he could reach his hair. He then began to braid the baboon's locks.

"Are you okay, my friend? I hope the braids do not hurt," the tortoise said kindly.

"It hurts a bit, I must confess, but as they say, no pain no gain."

"And you will be the envy of every animal in this region. I bet the lion will be asking me to weave his hair next."

Both of them laughed and the tortoise continued to weave Mulu's hair meticulously. He cleverly wove every inch into a long, sturdy tree branch. It was so tight that Mulu could hardly move.

An hour later, the tortoise announced, "I've finished now, but you must not move an inch until the hair is well settled."

"What does well settled mean?" Mulu asked anxiously.

The tortoise chose his words carefully. "Your hair is very long and quite soft, so I had to anchor it to a branch, so you must sit still for a few more minutes. I'd like to come down now, can you kindly pick me up from the tree branch and throw me on the floor. Your hands are long, so I won't be too far off the ground when you drop me."

Mulu, who did not know the terrible predicament that was about to befall him, helped Ijapa. As soon as the tortoise was safe on the ground, he pulled the stool off Mulu's feet and left him hanging from the tree. The Gelada's braided locks held him firmly onto the braches.

Mulu let out an ear-bursting yell, but the tortoise was already on his way home. It was a quiet morning and there were no animals in the area. The baboon tried to loosen his braids, but the more he tried, the worse the pain. In agony, he shouted, "wait until I get my hands on you, wicked tortoise. Ouch! I think my head is going to split in two!" Mulu was in so much pain that every word he uttered caused him more agony, so he winced and wriggled. Every second was like days, and the pain felt as if someone had set his whole body ablaze. He was about to give up when he heard a rustling sound above him.

"Who is there?" he managed feebly.

"Sh...sh... it's me."

"Who?"

"Leul."

"Prince Leul? What are you doing up there?

"We are nibbling at your braids to loosen them up so you can get off this branch and we..."

"We?"

"Well, I brought my mother's colony to help, so we can get the job done quickly; you look like you are about to faint."

"But you're ever so tiny, what can you..."

"That sounds very familiar, 'what can a tiny ant like you do for me?'"

"I'm so sorry I said that to you earlier, Leul. Still, a colony of ants cannot unravel what that wicked tortoise has done."

"Have some faith; all things are possible. By the way, you may be glad to know that we are making progress; so hang in there." Mulu prayed quietly and hoped that the ants could save his life; they were his last hope.

After what seemed like an eternity, Leul announced that there was only one row of braids left. Mulu was already feeling better; he couldn't thank his helpers enough.

"I am so grateful to you, Leul, you saved my life!"

"So we did."

"Yes, thank you everyone; I owe you my life. Wait until I get hold of that tortoise; he will curse the day he was born and he will…"

"Wait a minute," Leul interrupted. "What did you do to deserve this? Why does Ijapa want you dead?"

"All I did was eat his grass seeds when the famine was really bad. One day, I saw him carrying a sack of seeds and I asked for some… politely, but you know how selfish Ijapa is; he totally refused, so I helped myself."

Leul cut in. "If I hear you right, this is a revenge game."

"You call this a game?" asked Mulu angrily. "I would have died on this tree if not for you and your helpers! How could…"

"But you're now planning to go and look for the tortoise and take revenge when you get down from this torture chamber? When do you want to end the vicious circle?"

"And what would you suggest I do, Mr Wise Ant?"

"I suggest you let go of anger and get busy doing something useful. We ants are so preoccupied with the work we've been created to do that we have no time to take account of evil deeds or play the revenge game."

There was a lengthy silence between the two as the ants continued to unravel the last row of braids. At last, they successfully set Mulu free from his bondage and he thanked them profusely for saving his life. However, instead of carrying out his plan to take revenge on the tortoise, Mulu headed for the palace to tell the king about the kindness of Leul the prince and how he and the colony of ants had saved his life. The king invited Leul to the palace, gave him a chieftaincy title, and threw a party in his honour.

When the tortoise heard the news that the Gelada was safe, he quickly packed his meagre belongings and left the Simien Mountains. He was afraid that Mulu might hurt him. From that time on, he became a fugitive, moving from one place to another, in order to avoid Mulu, and he made sure that their paths never crossed again.

Today, you may see the nomadic Ijapa in lay-bys and bush paths in the lowlands. Sadly, he may never know that Mulu the Gelada baboon had forgiven him.

ABOUT THE AUTHOR
ABIMBOLA GBEMI ALAO

Abimbola is an author, lecturer, performing storyteller and a children's book translator. Her work includes the Yoruba translation of 'Hansel and Gretel', 'The Little Red Hen and the Grain of Wheat', and several other books published by Mantra Lingua. Abimbola is the author of 'The Legendary Weaver: New Edition', 'The Goshen Principle' and 'How to Enhance Your Storytelling With Music'. She is an award-winning playwright and her short play, 'Legal Stuff' won the BBC/Royal Court 24 Degrees Competition in 2008. She is also the founder of 'Story-Weavers for Dementia', a programme that uses a non-pharmacological approach for dementia care, and she is the compiler of 'Narrative Adventures from Plymouth Memory Café'.

OTHER BOOKS BY
ABIMBOLA GBEMI ALAO

**The Goshen Principle: A
Shelter in the Time of Storm**
By Abimbola Gbemi Alao

ISBN
Paperback: 9780954625511
Ebook: 9780954625559

**The Legendary Weaver:
New Edition**
By Abimbola Gbemi Alao

ISBN
9780954625528

How to Enhance Your Storytelling with Music
By Abimbola Gbemi Alao

ISBN
Paperback: 978-0-954625535
Ebook: 978-0-954625566

Dual Language books, translated by Abimbola Gbemi Alao

Floppy's Friends:
'Awon ore e Floppy'
Dual Language Yoruba
translation by Abimbola Alao.
(2004) Mantra Lingua.

ISBN
1 84444240 3

Hansel and Gretel:
'Hansel ati Gretel'
Dual Language Yoruba
translation by Abimbola Alao.
(2005) Mantra Lingua.

ISBN
1 84444778 2

The little Red Hen and the
Grains of Wheat: 'Adie Pupa
Kekere ati Eso Alikama'
Dual Language Yoruba
translation by Abimbola Alao.
(2005) Mantra Lingua.

ISBN
1 84444219 5

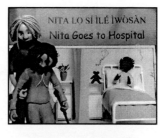

Nita Goes to Hospital:
'Nita lo si ile iwosan'
Dual Language Yoruba
translation by Abimbola Alao.
(2005) Mantra Lingua.

ISBN
1 84444836 3

Grandma's Saturday Soup:
'Obe Ojo Abameta Mama Agba'
Dual Language Yoruba
translation by Abimbola Alao.
(2005) Mantra Lingua.

Welcome to the world baby:
'Kaabo sinu aye Omo titun'
Dual Language Yoruba
translation by Abimbola Alao.
(2005) Mantra Lingua.

ISBN
1 84444951 3

ISBN
1 84444297 7

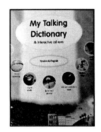

My Talking Dictionary &
Interactive CD ROM
Yoruba & English – Yoruba
translation by Abimbola Alao.
(2005) Mantra Lingua.

ISBN
1 84444717 0